OVER the NET

BY JAKE MADDOX

illustrated by Tuesday Mourning

text by Val Priebe

Impact Books are published by Stone Arch Books
151 Good Counsel Drive, P.O. Box 669
Mankato, Minnesota 56002
www.stonearchbooks.com

Library of Congress Cataloging-in-Publication Data
Maddox, Jake.

    Over the Net / by Jake Maddox; illustrated by Tuesday Mourning.

    p. cm. — (Impact Books. A Jake Maddox Sports Story)

    ISBN 978-1-4342-1213-9 (library binding)

    ISBN 978-1-4342-1403-4 (pbk.)

    [1. Volleyball—Fiction. 2. Self-confidence—Fiction.] I. Mourning,
Tuesday, ill. II. Title.
PZ7.M25643Ov 2009
[Fic]—dc22   2008031959

Summary:
Allie loves everything about volleyball – except hitting. She doesn't think
she's good at it, and every time she messes up, her belief in her own
abilities dwindles. Finally, she asks for help. Her idol, Nikki, agrees to
coach her once a week. If Allie can learn to spike as well as she blocks,
she could become one of the team's strongest players.

Creative Director: Heather Kindseth
Graphic Designer: Carla Zetina-Yglesias

Photo Credits:
iStock/Nancy Louie, cover (background), 1 (background)

1 2 3 4 5 6 14 13 12 11 10 09

Table of
CONTENTS

Chapter 1

BAD
PRACTICE

The gym was filled with the sounds of bouncing volleyballs and talking girls. Half of Allie's team was on one side of the net, and half was on the other.

Allie caught one ball as it sailed over the net. She stepped behind the line a few feet. Then she tossed the ball straight up into the air, about an arm's length in front of her. She stepped forward and swung her right arm forward to serve.

Just then, Coach Anderson blew her whistle. "Okay, girls, that's enough," she said.

Allie's serve hit the net. "Whoops!" she said under her breath.

"Okay, everyone!" called Coach loudly. "We're going to split up and work on skills. Hitters and setters, get to the net. Other players, go to the other side and get ready to receive. Go!"

Allie sighed. She was a hitter, but she had never been very good at it.

Her favorite part of volleyball was blocking. She loved to jump as high as she could, spread her hands out, and watch the ball hit them before it fell to the floor on the other side of the net. She especially loved the loud *smack* sound it made.

Spiking was her least favorite part of practice. She felt like everyone expected her to be the best at it, just because she was the tallest.

Allie felt like she was letting her team down when she didn't slam the ball to the floor on the other side of the net. It was even worse when she hit the ball into her team's side of the net and the other team scored a point.

Allie stood nervously at the back of the line of spikers. She looked up at the clock on the wall. It was 4:40.

At least I'll only have to do this for twenty more minutes, she thought. *I can handle it for that long.*

Soon, it was Allie's turn to hit. She took a deep breath.

Lizzie, the setter, pushed the ball up with her fingertips. It soared into the air and toward Allie. Allie took two hard steps to the net and jumped straight up.

She swung her right arm forward to hit the ball. But she didn't hear the loud *thunk* she wanted. Allie felt the ball hit the last two fingers on her right hand. Then the ball teetered on the edge of the net. Finally, it fell to the floor on the other side.

Allie tried to hit the next one, but it hit the net on her side. Lizzie called out, "It's okay!" But Allie could feel her face burning with embarrassment.

After taking a deep breath, Allie stepped up to try again.

Luckily, Coach Anderson blew her whistle. Practice was over.

"Huddle!" the coach shouted, like she did at the end of every practice. The team gathered around.

"Okay, team," Coach Anderson said. "Good work today! We'll have practice tomorrow as usual. Our match against Cooperville on Monday is at home, just like it says on the schedule. Also, summer league sign-ups will start on Monday. Anyone who is interested in playing on the freshman team next year needs to be in summer league." She smiled and added, "That's it. Have a good night!"

Allie's stomach dropped. She wanted to play next year. But how could she join the summer league or play on the freshman team when she couldn't even spike?

Chapter 2

QUITTING?

Allie barely tasted her dinner that night. After putting her dishes in the dishwasher, she went to her room and closed her door. She sat down at her desk and opened her algebra homework, but she wasn't really looking at it.

She just kept thinking about what Coach Anderson had said. The coach had said that anyone who wanted to play next year had to play summer league.

Of course Allie wanted to play next year! Volleyball was Allie's favorite sport in the world. She loved it. But she wouldn't even make it through tryouts for the freshman team if she couldn't spike the ball.

After a while, Allie managed to stop thinking about volleyball. She was even able to finish her algebra homework. As soon as she finished, she called her best friend, Kate.

"Hey," said Kate. "How was practice?"

"Awful!" exclaimed Allie. "I am such a bad player! I still can't spike the ball, and we're more than halfway through the season. Coach said today that we need to sign up for summer league if we want to play next year. I really want to play, but what's the point? I'm the tallest player. It's embarrassing if I can't spike the ball!"

Allie stopped talking. She was almost in tears.

Kate sighed. "Allie, calm down," she said. "You're not a bad player. You know that! There is just one part of the game you need to work on. We've talked about this so much. I just wish you'd believe that you're good at volleyball."

"I know," Allie said. "Me too."

"Look, you have a coach for a reason, right?" asked Kate. "She's there to help you get better. So tomorrow after practice, why don't you just ask her for help?"

Allie wanted to tell Kate she thought that was a bad idea. But she stopped. She frowned and thought for a minute. Maybe Kate was right. Maybe Allie just needed to ask for help.

"Are you still there?" Kate asked.

Allie smiled. "Yeah, just thinking," she said. "I think you might be right. I'll talk to Coach Anderson tomorrow."

"Great!" Kate said. "I'm glad to hear that you're not giving up. You're no quitter, Allie! You'll be a great spiker before you know it."

"Yeah, maybe," Allie said. She just couldn't stop thinking about that day's volleyball practice and the two spikes she'd messed up.

Chapter 3

UNEXPECTED HELP

The next afternoon, practice was terrible again. Allie practiced hitting, but she couldn't get anything over the net.

Just as she was starting to think she'd never be more embarrassed, she heard a familiar voice. "Come on, Allie! You can do it!" someone yelled.

Allie's stomach dropped when she realized who was yelling. It was Nikki, Allie's favorite varsity volleyball player.

Nikki was a junior in high school. She was the best hitter on the varsity team — maybe in the whole state.

Allie had been to all of the varsity team's home matches. She'd watched Nikki hit the ball straight down to the floor over and over again. Nikki was amazing.

So when Allie was messing up every single hit of her own, Nikki was the last person Allie wanted to be watching. She felt her cheeks burning.

Luckily, just then, Coach Anderson finally blew her whistle. She called the team in for the end-of-practice huddle.

"Great work today, girls," said Coach Anderson. "Have a good weekend. Remember, our match on Monday is at home. See you then!"

Everyone started to head to the locker room, but Allie hung back. Then she walked across the gym to Coach Anderson's office. She knocked on the half-open door.

"Come in!" called Coach Anderson.

Allie pushed the door open. "Hey, Allie!" Coach Anderson said. "What's up?"

Allie looked down at the floor. Standing in the doorway, she quietly said, "Coach, I was wondering if you could help me with my hitting. I really want to play on the freshman team next year, and I'm afraid I won't make the team if I can't learn to spike."

She looked up, hoping to see Coach Anderson's reaction. To her surprise, she saw Nikki sitting in a chair against the wall. Coach Anderson smiled at Allie.

"Oh!" exclaimed Allie. "I didn't know you were busy. I'm really sorry!" She started to back out of the office. "I'll just talk to you next week," she added.

"Wait, Allie! I'm not busy," exclaimed Coach. "Nikki's just here visiting."

"I had to bring some stuff down from the varsity coach," explained Nikki. "You know, for summer league sign-ups and stuff."

"Oh, yeah," said Allie. She smiled and tried to stop feeling embarrassed.

"To answer your question, Allie, I would be more than happy to help you with your hitting," said Coach Anderson. "I am very proud of you for asking for help. And I'm very happy that you want to keep playing next year." She paused and looked at Allie.

Allie felt relieved, but she still felt nervous. "I love volleyball," she said quietly.

"I know you do," Coach Anderson said. She went on, "Like I was saying, I'd be happy to help you with hitting. But I think I know someone else who is much more qualified to give you the help you want."

Coach Anderson looked at Nikki and raised her eyebrows. "How about it, Nikki?" the coach asked. "I've always been a setter. What Allie really needs is another hitter to help her. Do you want to be her coach?"

Nikki smiled at Allie. "I would love to!" she said brightly.

"Great!" said Coach. "Well, maybe we can get started this weekend. Can you both be here tomorrow morning at 10?"

"Yeah, I can," Nikki said.

Allie nodded. "Me too," she said.

Coach Anderson smiled. "Then it's settled," she said. "I'll see you both here tomorrow morning at 10."

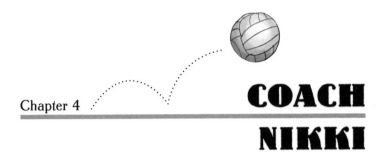

Chapter 4

COACH

NIKKI

Allie usually slept in on Saturdays. This Saturday was different.

Allie woke up a lot earlier than she normally would have. She was nervous, but she was surprised to realize that she was really looking forward to practicing with Nikki.

Nikki and Coach were already in the gym when Allie's mom dropped her off.

"Good morning, Allie!" said Nikki when Allie walked in. "Are you ready to get to work?"

"Yeah," said Allie. "Teach me everything you know."

Nikki laughed. "Whoa," she said. "Let's just start with spiking, okay?"

"Sounds great," Allie said. She already felt more relaxed.

"Why don't we run a few laps to get warmed up?" Nikki suggested. "Then we'll start working on hitting."

Coach Anderson smiled. "I think you're in good hands, Allie," she said. "If you guys need me, I'll be in my office."

"Okay!" Allie said. Coach Anderson walked across the gym to her office. Allie turned to Nikki.

"Let's get started," Nikki said.

First, Allie and Nikki ran three laps around the gym. Then they stretched out their arms and shoulders.

"Okay," Nikki said when they were warmed up. "Why don't you show me how you normally start out when you're hitting?"

"Why?" Allie asked. "I'm pretty sure I'm not doing it right."

"Well, let's see," Nikki said.

Allie showed Nikki how she did her approach when she was hitting. She started behind the ten-foot line, stepped forward with her left foot, took another step with her right foot, and jumped forward a little toward the net. Her right arm was bent at the elbow.

After Nikki watched Allie, she said, "Well, I can see a few places where you can improve your approach."

"Like what?" Allie asked.

"Well, you're right-handed, right?" Nikki began.

Allie nodded. Nikki went on, "That means you should start with your right foot. First, take two really hard, fast steps. Your third step, with your right foot, should be in the air, kind of like a lay-up in basketball. Does that make sense?"

Allie followed Nikki's direction. It did make sense. In fact, Allie had never heard the approach explained that way before. She was learning already!

"You're a really good blocker, right?" Nikki asked.

Allie smiled. "Yeah," she said. "I really like to block. It's fun."

"Great!" exclaimed Nikki. "Hitting isn't that much different than blocking. To be a good hitter, you need to jump straight up in the air, just like blocking. The most important part is to keep your eyes on the ball the whole time."

"I can do that," said Allie.

By the time practice was over, Allie was tired and sweaty. Her head was swimming with everything Nikki had told her, but she really felt like she had gotten better.

"So, same time next week?" Nikki said, smiling.

"That would be great," Allie said. "See you then!"

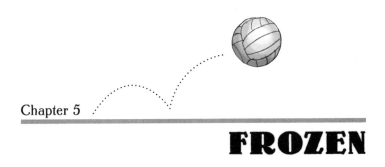

Chapter 5

FROZEN

On Monday, Allie was nervous for that night's volleyball match. But she was excited to try out the new techniques she'd learned. The school day went by quickly.

After school, she hung out with Kate until the other team's bus arrived. Then she headed into the locker room to get ready.

Allie was nervous. Still, she was trying to act normal.

After all, she loved playing volleyball. Games were usually really fun. As long as the hitting part went well, she'd be fine.

At first, everything was great. All of Allie's serves went over the net. In the second game of the match, she made two good blocks. But then the players rotated. That brought Allie to her turn at the net. It was her turn to spike.

"Allie!" Lizzie called. "Your ball."

Allie looked up. The ball was speeding toward her.

Allie froze. Her mind went completely blank. She couldn't remember anything that Nikki had taught her at Saturday's practice. It seemed like time was standing still.

I can't do it, she thought.

She looked up just in time to see the ball coming down toward her. It was too late.

She tried to jump straight up, like Nikki had said, but she took her eyes off the ball. When she hit it, she hit it straight into the net.

Her team had already used their three hits, so the other team got a point. All of Allie's confidence from the beginning of the game had disappeared, just like the things she'd learned from Nikki.

A minute later, Coach stood up, signaled to the referee for a substitution, and took Allie out of the game.

The team always rotated players. Allie knew it was just her turn to come out, but she couldn't help feeling like it was also because she had really messed up.

She walked to the bench and sat down. As she looked under the bench for her water bottle, she heard Coach Anderson call, "Allie!"

"Yeah?" Allie replied.

"Come talk to me for a minute," said Coach Anderson. Allie bent to pick up her water bottle and walked back down the bench to sit next to Coach.

"What's up, Coach?" asked Allie. Her voice shook. She was afraid she was going to get into trouble for her mistake.

"I wanted to make sure you knew that I only took you out because it was your turn," said Coach. "You looked upset."

"Yeah," replied Allie. She looked down at the floor. "I know. I'm just upset with myself. I thought I did so well at practice."

"First of all, you did do well at practice with Nikki. And secondly, everyone makes mistakes, Allie," Coach Anderson said. "One practice with Nikki isn't going to fix everything. Nikki's been playing for years. But keep up your hard work. It'll come." Coach smiled. She gave Allie a pat on the back.

Allie nodded and took a drink from her water bottle. She wanted to believe that Coach Anderson was right. But she wasn't so sure.

Chapter 6

UPS AND DOWNS

Allie didn't talk to Coach Anderson about her spiking for the rest of the week. She felt too embarrassed and disappointed in herself.

She just wanted to pretend that Monday's match hadn't happened. The less Allie had to think about it, the better she seemed to play. But whenever Allie remembered what had happened, she played really badly.

On Saturday morning, Allie met Nikki at school again.

"Let's run a few laps again, Allie," said Nikki. "Then we'll get right to work."

"Sounds good, Coach Nikki," said Allie. "I'm ready to get started."

After they ran laps and stretched, Nikki said, "So, Allie, Coach Anderson told me what happened at your match on Monday."

Allie felt her face heat up. "She did?" Allie asked.

"Yeah. And I wanted to tell you, it's not a big deal," said Nikki.

"Yes it is," Allie said. "Why? I froze up and hit the ball right into the net. I let the other team score."

Nikki smiled at Allie. "I know that feeling," Nikki said. "Believe me, I know. But we only had one practice together. And it was only one point."

"I guess," Allie said. She started to feel a little bit better.

"Besides," continued Nikki. "You won the match, right? Coach said you had some awesome blocks. She also said that you served really well."

"She did? Cool," Allie said. Then she frowned. "I just wish I hadn't made that mistake."

"I make mistakes all the time," Nikki said. "Everyone does. The key is not to let one mistake ruin the rest of your game. You just have to let it go and get your mind back on the next play."

"Really?" Allie asked. "Even when it's a really bad mistake?"

"Yes," Nikki said firmly. "Everyone has their ups and downs. It's part of playing the game. Now, let's run through your approach a few times, and then we'll start hitting."

Allie was quiet as they started working on her approach. For the second Saturday in a row, what Nikki had said made sense. And for the second Saturday in a row, Allie felt more confident in herself.

* * *

The next match was on Tuesday afternoon. Just like she had at the match the week before, Allie started to feel nervous when she realized that it was her turn to spike.

The more she worried about letting down her teammates and disappointing her coach, the worse she felt. All of the confidence Allie had gotten during practice with Nikki was gone.

Lizzie called, "Allie!"

Allie looked up. The ball was headed toward her.

Just like Nikki had taught her, Allie took three steps, jumped, and swung. But at the very last second, she closed her eyes. The ball fell to the floor right next to her.

The girls from the other team cheered and laughed. "Someone's scared of the ball!" one of the girls said.

Allie's teammates patted her on the back. "Don't worry about it," Lizzie said. "You'll get the next one."

Allie felt like she was going to cry. She looked over at Coach Anderson, who was sitting on the bench.

Coach gave her a kind look, stood up, and motioned to the official for a substitution.

Chapter 7

LAST PRACTICE

That Saturday was Nikki and Allie's last practice together. Allie's team was playing their last match of the season on Tuesday.

The varsity team was getting ready for the state volleyball tournament. That meant Nikki would have to practice with her own team on Saturdays.

Nikki and Allie began practice. First, they stretched out their shoulders.

As they stretched, Nikki said, "I don't think my varsity Saturday practices are going to be as much fun as these." She glanced at Allie and smiled.

Allie didn't smile back. "At least at those practices you'll actually be doing some good," she said.

"What do you mean?" asked Nikki, frowning. "Aren't our practices helping you? You always do so great when we're here. I really think you've improved a lot!"

"I know," said Allie. "This has helped me a lot. When it's just us, I do great. But then when it's time to hit in a real match, I don't know." She paused and bit her lip. Then she said quietly, "When I'm playing for real, I just sort of freeze up, and I can't remember anything you've taught me."

Coach Anderson walked up. "Does that sound familiar, Nikki?" she asked, sitting down next to the two girls.

Nikki gave a short laugh. "Yeah," she said, shaking her head. "It does. It sounds really familiar."

"What do you mean? What sounds familiar?" asked Allie, confused.

Coach Anderson and Nikki looked at each other. Coach smiled and said, "I'll let you tell her all about it, Nikki." She stood up. She added, "I'm going to my office to do some paperwork. Just let me know if you need anything." Coach walked away.

When Coach Anderson had left the gym, Allie turned to Nikki. "What's she talking about? Tell me all about what?" asked Allie.

Nikki sighed. Then she smiled and said, "Okay, here's the story." She took a deep breath. Then she went on, "Coach Anderson was my eighth grade coach too. And when I was in eighth grade, I was the tallest girl on my team."

"Just like me," Allie said.

Nikki smiled. "Yes, exactly like you," she said. "And, just like you, I also had a really hard time spiking."

Allie couldn't believe what she was hearing. Nikki couldn't hit when she was in eighth grade? But she had won every award possible for being one of the best hitters in high school.

Allie shook her head. "You're just trying to make me feel better," she said. "You're the best hitter on varsity! There's no way you were ever not good at spiking."

Nikki smiled and said, "Thanks, Allie. But I'm telling you the truth. Just ask Coach Anderson. I used to have the same problems being confident that you have now. Especially about spiking."

"Then how did you get so good?" asked Allie. "What's the secret?"

Nikki shrugged. She said, "I practiced every day. I even had extra practice with my older sister. She was the best. And I just kept telling myself that I could do it."

Nikki paused, looking at Allie's face. Then she continued, "It took kind of a long time. And I still had bad matches and practices and stuff sometimes. That's normal. But I just kept trying. I really love volleyball, and I couldn't imagine not playing anymore."

"That's exactly how I feel! " exclaimed Allie. "I love volleyball. And I really want to keep playing. I just don't know if I'm good enough."

"You are good enough," Nikki said. "And you should keep working hard. Keep pushing yourself and keep telling yourself that you can do it. If you believe you can do it, you'll be able to do it. Seriously, I know it sounds really cheesy, but it's true."

She smiled at Allie. Then Nikki asked, "Now, are you ready to practice?"

Allie took a deep breath and looked at Nikki. "Yes, I am," Allie said.

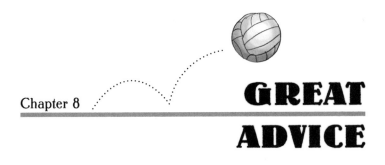

Chapter 8

GREAT ADVICE

Allie looked out her bedroom window on the morning of the last volleyball match of the season. It was cloudy and rainy outside. *Great*, she thought. *I hope this isn't the sign of a really bad day.*

As she got ready for school, Allie thought about what Nikki had said at their last practice. Nikki had seemed so sure that all Allie needed to do was believe she could do it.

Easier said than done, Allie thought as she walked downstairs for breakfast.

She dropped her duffle bag and backpack by the kitchen table. She flopped into a chair with a sigh.

Allie's mom raised her eyebrows and asked, "Is something wrong, honey? You seem stressed."

"No," said Allie. "Not really. I'm just nervous. It's the last match today. I just want to do well."

"Just do your best," said Mom. "You know what they say — if you believe you can do something, you will be able to do it." She smiled at Allie.

"Yeah, that's what I hear," Allie said.

* * *

At lunch, Allie sat with Kate.

"So, how's everything going?" asked Kate. "Are you nervous about the game tonight?"

"I don't know," said Allie. She ate a tater tot. Then she went on, "I'm kind of sad that it's the last match for this year. And I'm really nervous about how I'm going to do. Are you coming?"

"Of course I'm coming! I wouldn't miss it!" said Kate, smiling at her friend. "And don't be nervous. Here's a trick I learned for when I'm in a play and I'm scared. I just tell myself to believe that I'm the person I'm playing. Then I'm not as nervous. So you should just tell yourself, 'I'm Allie, the awesome volleyball player.' And you'll feel way better!"

Allie smiled. "That's great advice, Kate," she said. "Thanks."

* * *

After school, Allie sat by her locker doing homework while she waited for the other school's bus to show up. She had her math book open in front of her, but she was having a really hard time paying attention.

More than once, she caught herself staring at the wall on the other side of the hallway. She just kept thinking about all of those Saturday practices with Nikki. Had she really learned anything?

Allie sighed. She still hadn't decided if she would sign up for summer league yet. She knew she had to sign up if she wanted to play next year.

For about the hundredth time that season, Allie thought about how much she wanted to play volleyball the next year. She'd always planned to play when she was a freshman.

Volleyball was her favorite thing. She loved blocking, and she liked serving. Plus, playing as a freshman would mean spending time in practices and at games with Nikki, who would be a senior next year.

The problem was, Allie didn't know if she would make the team without being able to spike. She could do everything else well. But was that enough?

She heard a large group of girls talking and giggling at the other end of the hall. It was time to get ready for the match.

Chapter 9

"I KNOW I CAN"

When she and the rest of her teammates walked into the gym to start doing their warm-ups, Allie looked at the bleachers. Her mom was there. She was sitting with Kate and Nikki, a few rows behind Allie's team's bench.

When they saw Allie looking at them, Kate, Nikki, and Mom pulled out a white sign. It read, "GO ALLIE!" in blue and gold, the school's colors.

For the first time, Allie started to feel like that day's match would be different. Before, she would have worried that Nikki would see her mess up or that she would make a mistake and disappoint her team. Today, though, Allie was happy and excited to see her friends and mom there to cheer her on.

She thought about the advice all three people had given her. *I can do it*, Allie thought. *I know I can.*

The first four games of the five-game match were very close. Allie's team won the first and fourth games. The other team won the second and third games.

Allie and her teammates really wanted to end their season with a win. It was their last eighth-grade game. Plus, it was the last game they'd ever play in that gym, where they'd played all through middle school.

In the fifth game, the score was 22–20. Allie's team was winning. And it was Allie's turn in the rotation to hit.

Three points, thought Allie. *I have to hang in here for three points. I can do it.*

It was Allie's team's turn to serve. The first serve went over the net.

Two players from the other team yelled, "Mine!" But both of them backed away, expecting the other girl to hit the ball. It hit the floor between the two girls.

Allie's team cheered. The other team's coach called for a time-out. Then both squads jogged to their benches.

Allie took a deep breath. *One point down*, she thought. *Just two more to go.*

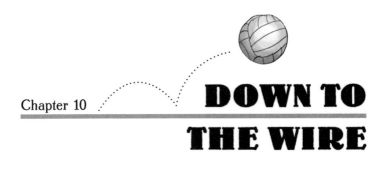

Chapter 10

DOWN TO
THE WIRE

When the time-out was over, Allie's team served again. This time, the other team returned the serve.

Someone in the back row on Allie's side bumped the ball into the air. It flew right to Lizzie, who tipped it just over the top of the net.

A girl from the other team dove for the ball, but she slid too far under the net. Allie's team had scored again!

Allie glanced up into the stands. All of the fans were excited. Kate, Nikki, and Mom were jumping up and down and cheering.

Allie caught Nikki's eye. Nikki yelled, "Just watch the ball! You can do it!" Allie smiled and gave her a thumbs-up. Then she took a deep breath and faced the net.

The next serve flew over the net. A girl from the other team called for the ball and bumped it to their setter. The setter called the name of their hitter. The hitter stepped forward, wound up, and spiked the ball over the net.

Allie's teammates were ready. The first hit headed toward Lizzie. Lizzie got ready. She spread her fingers wide to set the ball up for a spike.

Then Allie heard Lizzie call her name.

This time, Allie wasn't worried. She knew she had to make the hit. That was the only thing on her mind.

Just like Nikki had taught her, Allie didn't take her eyes off of the ball. She stepped forward with her right foot, then her left. She stuck out her arm. With her right foot still in the air, she jumped up and swung her right arm down onto the ball as hard as she could.

The ball hit the floor on the other side of the net. It made a loud noise that echoed through the gym. *Smack!* It was Allie's favorite sound.

The fans in the stands, the players on the bench, and Allie's teammates on the court all cheered and shouted.

Allie looked up at the stands. She could see her mom, Kate, and Nikki jumping up and down next to each other in the bleachers.

Allie smiled. She had done it! She had made a great hit! And her team had won!

After the game, Coach Anderson took Allie aside.

"That was a great game, Allie," said Coach. "I am really proud of you. You worked very hard this season, and your hard work has really paid off."

"Thanks, Coach," Allie said.

Coach went on, "Now, I still haven't gotten your sign-up slip for summer league. Are you going to turn that in?"

"Of course, Coach!" said Allie. "I can't wait to play this summer."

"And next year," said Nikki, walking up to them.

"Right," Allie said. "And next year. And the year after that, and the year after that . . ."

Smiling, she and Nikki walked off the court.

About the
AUTHOR

Val Priebe lives in Minneapolis, Minnesota with her two crazy wiener dogs, Bruce and Lily. Besides writing books, she loves to spend her time reading, knitting, cooking, and coaching basketball. Other books that Val has written in this series include *Full Court Dreams* and *Stolen Bases*.

About the
ILLUSTRATOR

When Tuesday Mourning was a little girl, she knew she wanted to be an artist when she grew up. Now, she is an illustrator who lives in Knoxville, Tennessee. She especially loves illustrating books for kids and teenagers. When she isn't illustrating, Tuesday loves spending time with her husband, who is an actor, and their son, Atticus.

GLOSSARY

approach (uh-PROCH)—the beginning part of a spike, in volleyball

confident (KON-fuh-duhnt)—having a strong belief in your own abilities

familiar (fuh-MIL-yur)—well-known or easily recognized

huddle (HUDDLE)—to gather together in a group

league (LEEG)—a group of sports teams

reaction (ree-AK-shuhn)—an action in response to another action

rotated (ROH-tayt-id)—took turns doing something

serve (SURV)—to begin play by hitting the ball

substitution (suhb-stih-TOO-shuhn)—a replacement

techniques (tek-NEEKS)—ways of doing something

varsity (VAR-sih-tee)—the highest-level team at a school

THE HISTORY OF VOLLEYBALL

In 1895, William G. Morgan created a game called mintonette. He worked at the YMCA in Massachusetts. Morgan created the game for older members of the YMCA.

In 1896, the game was renamed volleyball. The game quickly spread to YMCAs around the United States.

Throughout the years, volleyball has continued to change. In the beginning, teams could have as many players as they wanted on the court. Players could hit the ball unlimited times before hitting it over the net.

The rules are different now. Now, only six players are allowed on the court, and the ball can only be hit three times by a team.

Flo Hymna, Paula Weishoff, Logan Tom, Danielle Scott, and Steve Timmons are some indoor volleyball greats.

Since its start in 1895, volleyball has become one of the most popular sports in the world. Every week, about 800 million people participate in a volleyball game. Whether played in a back yard or in the Olympics, its popularity continues to grow.

Discussion
QUESTIONS

1. Allie asks her coach for help spiking. What else could she have done to get help and improve her skills?

2. Why does Allie keep losing her confidence during volleyball games?

3. Allie gets advice from lots of people during chapter 8. Who else could she have asked for advice?

Writing
PROMPTS

1. In this book, Allie really looks up to Nikki. Write about someone you admire. What do you admire about that person?

2. Allie loves volleyball, but at the beginning of this book, she has some problems. Write about a time you had a problem doing something you loved. What happened? How did you fix the problem?

3. At the end of this book, Allie plans to join the summer volleyball league. Write a story that begins when this book ends. What happens next?

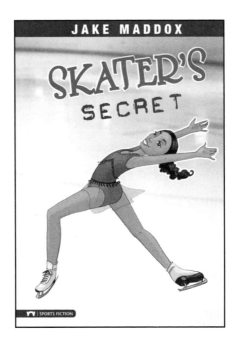

Maggie and Shannon are figure skaters and sisters. For once, Maggie is determined to come out from behind her sister's shadow. Can Maggie learn to shine, even when Shannon always seems to get in her way?

Molly has always dreamed of taking horseback
riding lessons, and now she is! Everything is
great . . . except that two girls at school keep
making fun of Molly. She'll need to figure out
a way to keep her confidence both in and out
of the saddle.

Internet
SITES

Do you want to know more about subjects related to this book? Or are you interested in learning about other topics? Then check out FactHound, a fun, easy way to find Internet sites.

Our investigative staff has already sniffed out great sites for you!

Here's how to use FactHound:

1. Visit *www.facthound.com*

2. Select your grade level.

3. To learn more about subjects related to this book, type in the book's ISBN number: **9781434212139**.

4. Click the **Fetch It** button.

FactHound will fetch the best Internet sites for you!